TO SERVE AND PROTECT

THE HISTORY OF POLICING

Law Enforcement and Intelligence Gathering

To Serve and Protect

The History of Policing

Edited by Lionel Pender

Britannica Educational Publishing

in association with

ROSEN

Educational Services

Published in 2017 by Britannica Educational Publishing (a trademark of Encyclopædia Britannica, Inc.) in association with The Rosen Publishing Group, Inc.
29 East 21st Street, New York, NY 10010

Distributed exclusively by Rosen Publishing.
To see additional Britannica Educational Publishing titles, go to rosenpublishing.com.

First Edition

Britannica Educational Publishing
J.E. Luebering: Director, Core Reference Group
Anthony L. Green: Editor, Compton's by Britannica

Rosen Publishing
Lionel Pender: Editor
Nelson Sá: Art Director
Brian Garvey: Designer
Cindy Reiman: Photography Manager
Karen Huang: Photo Researcher
Introduction and conclusion by Michael Ray.

Library of Congress Cataloging-in-Publication Data

Names: Pender, Lionel, editor.
Title: To serve and protect : the history of policing / edited by Lionel Pender.
Description: First edition. | New York, NY : Britannica Educational Publishing in association with The Rosen Publishing Group, Inc., 2017. | Series: Law Enforcement and Intelligence Gathering | Includes bibliographical references and index.
Identifiers: LCCN 2016020482 | ISBN 9781508103813 (library bound : alk. paper)
Subjects: LCSH: Police--History--Juvenile literature.
Classification: LCC HV7903 .T62 2017 | DDC 363.209--dc23
LC record available at https://lccn.loc.gov/2016020482

Manufactured in China

Photo credits: Cover, pp. 3, 30 Print Collector/Hulton Archive/Getty Images; pp. 8–9 Brian Vander Brug/Los Angeles Times/Getty Images; pp. 8–9 (background), 11, 25, 42, 67 hunthomas/Shutterstock.com; pp. 13, 14 Courtesy of the trustees of the British Museum; p. 16 Project Gutenberg (Text 10940); pp. 18, 36–37 Universal Images Group/Getty Images; p. 21 © Chronicle/Alamy Stock Photo; p. 23 DEA/G. Nimatallah/De Agostini Picture Library/Getty Images; p. 24 DEA Picture Library/Getty Images; p. 26 Kean Collection/Archive Photos/Getty Images; p. 28 Heritage Images/Hulton Archive/Getty Images; p. 31 London Stereoscopic Company/Hulton Archive/Getty Images; pp. 34–35, 49 Library of Congress Prints and Photographs Division; p. 40 Library of Congress, Washington, DC (Digital File Number: cph 3c09718); p. 44 © Everett Collection Inc./Alamy Stock Photo; p. 45 GraphicaArtis/Archive Photos/Getty Images; p. 47 Keystone/Hulton Archive/Getty Images; p. 51 FBI; p. 53 Margaret Bourke-White/The LIFE Picture Collection/Getty Images; pp. 55, 64–65, 70–71, 74–75, 80–81 © AP Images; p. 58 Bachrach/Archive Photos/Getty Images; p. 72 Eric Draper/The White House; pp. 78–79 Jewel Samad/AFP/Getty Images; back cover, interior pages (background) stefano carniccio/Shutterstock.com

CONTENTS

INTRODUCTION

The relationship between police and the people that they serve and protect has changed rather dramatically over the centuries. Perhaps more surprising, however, are the ways in which things have remained the same. The earliest societies used mediation to maintain peace and stability among their citizens. In the twenty-first century, at a time of increased scrutiny regarding the conduct of armed law-enforcement officers, such techniques were the focus of renewed interest. Peer intervention groups sought to "interrupt" the cycles that often fueled violent crime in urban areas, and these methods demonstrated some measure of success. Still, this model did not achieve widespread acceptance, and it still fell to police to enforce laws and to pursue those who broke them.

The professionalization of policing duties was a process that took centuries, and the creation of independent, civilian bodies of peace officers employed by the state is a relatively recent historical development. Enforcement of laws and community norms was done at the local, or even personal, level, and criminal investigations were left to those individuals—often the victims of the crimes themselves—who had the time and money to pursue them. Indeed, money would be a dominant factor in policing until the modern era, and the various systems of bounties, stipends, rewards, and patronage led to widespread abuse. Perhaps the most outrageous example of this was Jonathan Wild, an

Police officers patrol Los Angeles International Airport in California on March 22, 2016.

eighteenth-century British thief who organized a criminal network that stole items and resold them to their original owners.

Throughout much of history, military forces were often used as a primary or supplementary law-enforcement body. France created one of the earliest modern police forces in the sixteenth century when it enlisted former soldiers and officers to curtail the criminal activities of other disbanded soldiers in the French countryside. The centralized command and control structures that typify military organizations have both advantages and disadvantages when applied to law enforcement, however, and a body designed to ward against foreign threats is not necessarily suited to promote domestic harmony. One of the earliest British professional police forces was actually in Dublin, Ireland, and it functioned as much as an extension of London's will as a peacemaking body. In the United States, lawmakers explicitly forbade the use of the US military as a domestic law-enforcement body with the Posse Comitatus Act of 1878.

It was perhaps ironic, then, that the United States in the twenty-first century saw an increasing militarization of its local police forces, as surplus battlefield equipment from the wars in Iraq and Afghanistan trickled down to municipalities and aggressive policing techniques (including the use of deadly force) were employed for even minor offenses. These steps were taken in spite of a dramatic decline in the overall crime rate. The suicide hijackings of September 11, 2001, and subsequent attacks in London, Madrid, Paris, and Brussels saw an increased focus on international terrorism as a domestic law-enforcement issue, and local and national police forces struggled to achieve a balance between security and respect for the privacy—and indeed, the very lives—of law-abiding citizens.

Chapter One

FROM ANCIENT TIMES TO THE EARLY MODERN PERIOD

Policing can be broadly defined as practices meant to enforce common standards and to maintain order in a community. In this sense, policing is much older than the creation of any armed force specifically formed for such a task. The activity of policing existed for thousands of years before the introduction of police as a distinct body.

ANCIENT POLICING

The earliest civilizations found ways of enforcing laws and maintaining order. Sometimes law enforcement was in the hands of religious authorities or the military instead of political rulers. Some early police forces developed from the personal bodyguards of rulers or warlords. Occasionally, in the absence of a better means of preventing crime, groups of citizens in a community banded together for mutual protection. Often police in ancient civilizations performed various tasks, including garbage disposal and firefighting, that were not related to stopping crime.

The first police forces were created in Egypt in about 3000 BCE. Egypt then was divided into forty-two regions called nomes. Each of these regions had an appointed official who was responsible for justice and security. He was assisted by a chief of police, whose formal title was *sab heri seker*, meaning "chief of the hitters." (The hitters were a body of men who collected taxes, among other duties.)

In the city-states of ancient Greece, policing duties were assigned to magistrates. Different classes of magistrates had different responsibilities, some for city cleanliness, others for keeping order in the marketplace or enforcing standards of measure. A group known as the "Eleven" dealt with courts, prisons, and criminal justice. To carry out their duties, the magistrates depended in part on the military and also on a corps of 300 Scythian slaves purchased after the Greco-Persian Wars. Lightly armed, the Scythian slaves maintained peace and order in various public places.

Scythian archers, such as the one illustrated on this sixth-century-BCE plate by Epictetus, served as police in ancient Athens.

In Rome, one of the earliest well-regulated police forces was created under the emperor Augustus. In 7 BCE, he divided the city into 14 *regiones* (wards), each subdivided into *vici* (precincts). The precincts were overseen by magistrates responsible for fire protection and other administrative and religious duties. The following year, the fire brigade was expanded into a corps of seven squads of 1,000 men each. These squads were called the *vigiles*—those who kept watch (vigil) over the city. Each squad was responsible for fire protection and, especially at night, for police protection in two wards. As an additional measure, Augustus

The Roman emperor Augustus, portrayed in this first-century-CE bronze sculpture, instituted a well-regulated police force in ancient Rome.

created three squads of police under the command of a city prefect. In case of serious difficulty, the police could ask the assistance of the emperor's private bodyguard, the Praetorian Guard.

In 395, Rome split into Eastern and Western empires. After the fall of the Western Empire in the fifth century CE, the Eastern, or Byzantine, Empire kept some of the older Roman institutions. Among them was a police authority tasked with overseeing the large population of foreigners that resided in the capital, Byzantium (modern-day Istanbul, Turkey). Outside the Byzantine Empire, however, formal police bodies all but disappeared.

In Europe in the Middle Ages, police functions were carried out by servants of kings or nobles. As cities began to grow with the development of local commerce and manufacturing, the citizens were able to raise their own police forces. These were usually of a military character, since they were also needed to defend a city from outside attack. Most such city forces were raised from among local citizens and paid for by the merchants. As a consequence, they were often used to protect business interests from attack.

The legal codes produced during the early Middle Ages, such as the Salic Law, show that nearly all offenses were considered civil matters to be resolved informally between the parties involved. The conflict-solving methods established in England during this period offer a good example of how policing was done before modern police developed.

ENGLAND

Before the Norman Conquest of 1066, the Anglo-Saxons had a mutual-protection arrangement called frankpledge. It was a system of social obligation that made all adult males responsible for the good behavior of each other. Adult males were grouped into units called tithings, which consisted of ten men and their families. Each tithing, in turn, was grouped into a unit called a hundred, and each hundred was grouped into a shire. The shire was a political subdivision equivalent to the modern county.

King Clovis is shown dictating the Salic Law before his court in this facsimile of a miniature in the "Chronicles of St. Denis" manuscript, fourteenth century.

SALIC LAW

Salic Law was the law code of the Salian Franks, a powerful people of western Europe in the early Middle Ages. The code was issued around 507–511, late in the reign of Clovis, the founder of the Frankish kingdom. The Salic Law is mainly a penal and procedural code containing a long list of fines for various offenses and crimes. It also includes, however, some rules of civil law, such as a provision against female inheritance of property.

In its original form, the code is structurally of the pre-Christian era, the only one of the kind that exists. Other Germanic laws, such as those of the Visigoths and Burgundians, may be earlier in date but show considerable Christian influence. Despite the fact that it was first written down in Latin (after a long period of purely oral transmission), the Salic Law was very little influenced by Roman law. As a record of the Franks' early laws and customs, the Salic Law offers valuable clues about the conditions of early Germanic life and society.

Under the frankpledge system, when a crime occurred, a citizen would call together others and pursue the criminal. If there were no witnesses to a crime, the victim was responsible for finding out who the criminal was.

THE OFFICE OF CONSTABLE

The frankpledge system continued following the Norman Conquest, as private citizens were still given responsibility for watching over cities at night and for apprehending known offenders. However, the new rulers added the office of constable to the justice system. The title had been used in the Roman Empire as early as the fifth century. The constable was originally a member of the royal court—the "count of the stable" in charge of the king's horses. By the eleventh century in France, the constable had become one of the chief officials of state, with power over the king's cavalry. He also acquired judicial authority. Later he was given command of the army.

After the title of constable was introduced in England, its meaning continued to change. The English constable was originally a post in the royal court, but by the late thirteenth century, it had evolved into a local office. Local constables were given law-enforcement powers as assistants to sheriffs. Constables were responsible for putting down riots and violent crimes. Power to arm militias enabled them to carry out these functions.

King Edward I of England introduced the Statute of Winchester (1285), which legalized the frankpledge system and the various police posts that had developed over the previous centuries in England.

The sheriffs were local officials who performed a number of administrative tasks. The word "sheriff" comes from the words "shire" and "reeve." The reeve was an administrative official in charge of a shire. After 1066, when church courts were separated from state courts, sheriffs became the chief officials in counties and heads of courts. They were judges in both civil and criminal cases. Today's sheriffs are generally comparable to police chiefs and have no judicial powers.

In 1285, these law-enforcement arrangements were legalized in the Statute of Winchester. The act provided that it was a citizen's duty to maintain the peace, and any citizen could make an arrest. If offenders were not caught in the act, the citizen had to call together neighbors to hunt for them. All citizens were required to own weapons and participate in the chase if needed. A group of citizens engaged in pursuing criminals was called a "posse comitatus." Once caught, an offender was brought before the court by a constable. This system continued until the nineteenth century.

THIEFTAKERS

From the early sixteenth century in England, some groups of merchants, traders, church members, insurers, and others hired private individuals to protect them and their property. In addition, victims of theft offered rewards for the return of their stolen goods, often hiring "thieftakers." These were private citizens who, for a fee, attempted to identify wrongdoers and to return stolen property to its rightful owners.

As communities began paying private citizens to capture thieves, a standard set of fees was established, and a payment-based police system developed. Any citizen, not only constables and justices, could earn such fees and rewards by becoming a thieftaker or "common informer." During this period, constables and justices either were not paid at all or earned very little pay.

The fee-based system was subject to abuse by criminal networks. Perhaps the most successful of them was led by Jonathan Wild in the early eighteenth century. Wild organized the London underworld and arranged to have goods stolen so that he could sell them back to the original owners. After a seven-year reign as the "thieftaker general," Wild was caught and sent to the gallows.

FRANCE

From the early Middle Ages, France had a stronger and more effective system of policing than did England. It was organized, financed, and controlled by the government, and its chief purpose was to enforce the will

Jonathan Wild ran a successful criminal network in eighteenth-century London through which he arranged the theft of goods only to sell them back to their original owners.

of the king and his ministers. The police, in effect, were the personal force of the king.

Between 1536 and 1544, King Francis I instituted the first systematic measures to police France. He allocated police officials to the chiefs of his armies—the *maréchaux* ("marshals"). These military police roamed the countryside to catch offenders and used their sentencing power to inflict punishment, for which there was no appeal. These special forces came to be known collectively as the *maréchaussée*. Though effective in the countryside, the *maréchaussée* was not the answer to the problems afflicting France's cities—most notably the capital, Paris. To address this shortcoming, King Louis XIV created the first modern and efficient system of policing in Paris in 1666.

The order issued by Louis XIV created the office of lieutenant general of police. Nicolas de La Reynie, a magistrate, was the first person to hold the post, from 1667 to 1697. This reform brought the Paris police force under the authority of one office. The city was divided into twenty districts and policed by forty-eight commissioners of police. These officials had administrative and judicial authority. There were twenty police inspectors who investigated and collected information on crime and other activities within the districts. Police captains in charge of keeping order were assisted by foot soldiers, brigades of archers, horsemen,

In the sixteenth century, King Francis I implemented the first systematic measures to police France. He created the *maréchaussée*, a military police force that roamed the countryside to catch and punish offenders.

In 1667, Nicolas de La Reynie became the first lieutenant general of police in France, giving him command over the entire police force of Paris.

and others on city patrol. By 1750, the commissioners commanded more than 1,000 troops. This number grew to more than 3,000 in the years preceding the French Revolution. In 1788, Paris had one police officer for every 193 inhabitants. There was also a system of secret police to spy on all citizens.

Chapter Two

DEVELOPMENTS IN THE 18TH AND 19TH CENTURIES

Although England's system of social obligation remained in place for more than eight hundred years, it had serious weaknesses. Its flaws only became worse as a result of the Industrial Revolution and the rapid city growth that accompanied it. The system had become corrupted, especially in cities. The status of constables declined over the years, and few desired to hold the post.

Reformers in England began to call for the creation of a permanent body of men who would be in charge of policing under the higher authority of the state. For a model some looked to France. The French system also provided a model for other countries of Europe. The English system, in turn, influenced early policing in the United States.

FRANCE AFTER THE REVOLUTION

After the French Revolution of 1789, the police force of Paris was reorganized. It still had political responsibilities, mainly in preventing any threats to the revolution. The Ministry of Police was created in 1796. Joseph Fouché was appointed head of the police in 1799. He greatly strengthened the power of the police, and in a few years he was the most powerful man in France after Napoleon I.

Joseph Fouché was appointed head of the French police in 1799. In that post he became the second most powerful figure in France—behind only Napoleon.

In 1810, the investigative department of the police force, named the Sûreté, was formed by François-Eugène Vidocq. An ex-convict himself, Vidocq believed in using former criminals to catch criminals. He was the first of the modern detectives, and after his retirement he founded the first private detective agency. His exploits and writings inspired the creation of a new type of fiction, the detective story.

THE DEVELOPMENT OF PROFESSIONAL POLICING IN ENGLAND

At the same time that France was organizing its police forces, England's urban policing system was falling apart. Underpaid public constables had to rely on private thieftakers to maintain an appearance of law and order. By the late eighteenth century, serious crime and rioting had reached intolerable levels in English cities.

One of the early and unofficial attempts by Londoners to police themselves appeared in 1749. The Bow Street Runners were founded by the brothers John and Henry Fielding, both of whom served as magistrates at Bow Street Court. The organization patrolled the highways and streets within the parish of Bow Street. In 1762, the Bow Street Horse Patrol was added to

Founded in 1749, the Bow Street Runners were one of the earliest attempts by Londoners to create an organized police force in their city. The Bow Street Police Court is shown in this 1808 illustration.

combat the bands of highway robbers who worked the roads leading into the city.

A different type of police force was created in London in 1798 by the West India Trading Company. (It was about this time that the word "police" came into English usage.) London was at that time the largest port in the world, and thefts from shipping had grown to unmanageable proportions. The Thames River Police, as the organization was known, was meant to stop these thefts. The force was directed by Patrick Colquhoun, a Scottish economist who wrote treatises on policing. It had a full-time staff of 80 men and a volunteer staff of more than 1,100 who could be called on when needed. The Thames River Police patrolled along the river, hoping by their presence to prevent criminal activity. They were paid regular salaries and forbidden to accept fees or gratuities (unofficial payments) for their work. So successful was this experiment that Parliament put the Thames River Police on the public payroll.

In spite of the success of the Bow Street Runners and the Thames River Police, public opinion still opposed the formation of a standing police force in London. A police force would require public funding, and raising taxes was not popular. In addition, provincial leaders viewed urban crime and corruption as "London" problems. Finally, political leaders throughout England feared that a police force may ultimately be used for political purposes.

Significantly, however, English politicians already had instituted one standing police force—in Ireland, in response to challenges to English rule there in the 1780s. The Dublin Police Act of 1786 created a professional police force in Dublin (then the second largest city in the British Isles) consisting of forty horse police and four hundred constables. The creation of the force encountered great resistance at first. By 1812, however, when Robert Peel was appointed chief secretary for Ireland, Dublin was considered relatively free of crime.

PATRICK COLQUHOUN, THE ARCHITECT OF MODERN POLICING

By the late eighteenth century, political leaders and writers were calling for reforms to the London police system. In 1796, the Scottish economist Patrick Colquhoun published *A Treatise on the Police of the Metropolis*, in which he applied business principles to police administration. Colquhoun also wrote *A Treatise on the Functions and Duties of a Constable*, which may be his most novel book. Its crucial innovation was its emphasis on the personal qualities needed to be a constable—notably, efficiency and zeal. Colquhoun also stressed the need for police integrity and other moral virtues. He is considered the architect of modern policing.

Patrick Colquhoun

Later, as home secretary, Peel sponsored the Metropolitan Police Act of 1829. It created the London Metropolitan Police Department, the first professional police force in England. Since he was considered the founder of the force, the officers have long been called bobbies (Bobby is a nickname for Robert). The police force was assigned to work in the London area except for the City of London itself—the square mile of territory within the city that is today the financial district. The 1829 act stipulated that all police be in uniform. They were to be paid regular salaries and were not allowed to accept

Robert Peel set up the first disciplined police force for London in 1829. At center in this photograph is one of London's bobbies, shown on duty in about 1896.

any other payment for services or returned stolen property. This early police force also performed other tasks, including watching for fires and lighting streetlamps.

The London police soon proved themselves a capable crime-fighting force. Public acceptance grew. In 1835, Parliament passed the Municipal Corporations Act, calling on every borough to set up a police force under the control of a local watch committee. A police force for the City of London was created in 1839. In 1856, Parliament ordered the establishment of police forces in all provinces through the County and Borough Police Act. In 1842, London's Metropolitan Police created the first detective branch, which became the Criminal Investigation Department in 1878. In 1883, a unit was set up to deal with illegal political activities. Headquarters of the Metropolitan Police were in Scotland Yard.

EARLY POLICE IN THE UNITED STATES

The United States inherited England's common law and its system of social obligation. From the colonial era until well after the American Revolution, police work was done mainly by citizens. There were night watches to look out for fires and suspicious activities. Some towns elected sheriffs or constables after the English pattern. A general opposition to establishing regular government-sponsored police forces lasted until nearly the middle of the nineteenth century. New York City started the first permanent police force in the United States in 1844, and by the mid-1850s, most major American

VIGILANTES

In the frontier regions of the United States in the late eighteenth century, there arose a new form of the old Saxon tradition of frankpledge: the vigilante. In areas where formal police groups did not exist, it was not uncommon for citizens—sometimes called "regulators"—to band together in "committees of vigilance" to combat rampant crime or corruption. One such group, the Regulators of North Carolina, arose in the western frontier counties of that state in the 1760s. Opposed to the high taxes and corruption of the colonial government, the group sought vainly to obtain reforms; it then refused to pay taxes, agitated against public officials, and committed acts of violence. The Regulator insurrection was finally crushed by North Carolina governor William Tryon's colonial militia at the Battle of Alamance (May 16, 1771).

Another notable vigilante group, the San Francisco Committee of Vigilance, formed in the 1850s after gold discoveries in California brought rapid population growth to San Francisco, accompanied by an increase in violent crime. The committee's operations were characterized by arbitrariness and lack of due process.

In this illustration, New York City police officers break up a draft riot in 1863. Early American police forces were modeled on the London Metropolitan Police.

cities had police forces. Those early departments all used the London Metropolitan Police as a model. The first

unit of state police, the Texas Rangers, was established in 1835. Few other state police organizations were founded until after World War I.

From the beginning, American city police forces were highly decentralized. Their loyalties were to those who hired them and appointed their officers—the local political machines. Decentralization had the advantage of keeping police in close contact with their neighborhoods, which aided them in seeing potential trouble spots. Police knew local residents and were often recruited from among them. This personalized approach aided police in spotting troublemakers, identifying local problems, and providing various public services. It also led to the creation of the myth of the "tough street cop" who handled all problems on his beat through the application of physical punishment. This image still dominates police lore and media portrayals in the United States.

Decentralization also had its disadvantages. It exposed police to the same levels of corruption that were beginning to pervade the cities as a whole. It also hindered law enforcement because criminals observed no boundaries. They could easily flee the jurisdiction of a police force, and there was little cooperation between forces. Because of crime waves in the late 1800s, some states allowed corporations to form their own police forces. On many occasions, company police were used to break labor strikes.

The most famous independent police force was Pinkerton's National Detective Agency, founded by Allan Pinkerton in 1850. Pinkerton had immigrated to the United States from Scotland in 1842 and settled in Chicago, Illinois. After serving as deputy sheriff in Kane and Cook Counties, he resigned to form his agency. It specialized at first in protecting trains from theft and in antilabor activities. During the American Civil War, Pinkerton worked as a spy against the South. After the Civil War, one of his detectives, James McParlan, was

In the late 1800s, city police and private police forces were often tasked with breaking up labor strikes, such as this 1886 strike by streetcar employees in New York City.

Founded in 1850, Pinkerton's National Detective Agency was the most famous private police force in the nineteenth-century United States. The agency's motto was "We never sleep."

instrumental in breaking up the Molly Maguires, a terrorist organization that carried out crimes in the coalfields of Pennsylvania.

The first detective units in US cities were established in Boston in 1846, New York City in 1857, and Chicago in 1861. They were modeled on the detective branch established by the London Metropolitan Police in 1842. The personnel of these units were frequently former constables and other thief catchers who had worked basically as bounty hunters—they were paid fees for catching criminals. This policy, when continued by a detective unit, easily bred corruption. Several investigative units had to be disbanded and reorganized after major police scandals in a number of cities.

In the late nineteenth century, as immigrant groups slowly gained political control of city neighborhoods, the link between the police and neighborhood politics became closer. This led to political and financial corruption and injustice. Police became involved in political activity to ensure the election of certain candidates. They also accepted gratuities for not enforcing unpopular laws and excluded strangers from social and political life. By the end of the nineteenth century, citizens in many American cities were trying to reform police forces. Their goal was the creation of professional police forces that operated independently of political interference.

AUSTRALIA

Australia was settled as a British penal colony in 1788. The earliest law enforcement in Australia followed the English system, consisting of private citizens functioning as a watch system or as constables. This situation created serious problems, because many who were meant to enforce the law were drawn from the convicts who had been sent from England to populate the colony. City police forces were established after passage in 1833 of the Sydney Police Act, which was modeled on London's Metropolitan Police Act. In 1838, each of the six states created its own police agency.

CANADA

Because Canada was colonized by both France and England, two traditions of police work were in operation

Here, a man is shown serving with the North West Mounted Police (later called the Royal Canadian Mounted Police), Yukon Territory, Canada, c. 1917.

during part of the eighteenth century. Quebec city patterned its police after those in Paris, while Upper Canada (later Ontario) used the British constabulary arrangement. After 1759 (and victory in the Seven Years' War), the British imposed their system on the French areas. City departments were founded in Toronto in 1835, in Quebec city in 1838, and in Montreal in 1840. The first provincial police forces were established in 1867.

Canada's best-known police agency, the Royal Canadian Mounted Police (RCMP), was founded in 1873 as the North West Mounted Police. Its responsibilities were to maintain control over the sparsely populated western plains region. In contrast to other Canadian police forces, the RCMP is more like a military unit. Since 1920, when the force was renamed, it has been Canada's federal law-enforcement agency.

Chapter Three

DEVELOPMENTS IN POLICING SINCE 1900: THE UNITED STATES EXAMPLE

The struggle for political control of police in the United States gave rise to a new strategy of policing that spread internationally in the twentieth century. The strategy involved new managerial techniques, integrated sources of authority, innovative tactics, and a narrowed definition of police work. Many of the reform leaders were police administrators who wanted to make policing more professional. They sought to improve the administration and organization of their departments while at the same time isolating them from the corrupting influence of local politics.

This approach eventually led to the rejection of the idea that effective policing needed community approval and support. Instead, it emphasized crime fighting as the primary function of police work. The growing disconnect between police and community would have disastrous consequences in later decades.

FEDERAL AND STATE POLICE

As local police departments struggled with inefficiency and corruption in the early twentieth century, the federal and state governments created their own police organizations to assist with law enforcement. The first federal agency, the United States Secret Service, had been established in 1865 as a division of the Department of the Treasury to combat the rampant counterfeiting of US currency. The agency greatly reduced the use of fraudulent banknotes, and subsequently it was put in charge of policing other federal crimes, including smuggling and the production of illegal liquor. Beginning in the 1890s, the Secret Service was sometimes given the added responsibility of guarding the president. This duty was made permanent after the assassination of President William McKinley in 1901.

The Bureau of Investigation—which would later become the Federal Bureau of Investigation (FBI)—was founded within the Department of Justice in 1908. When the new agency was proposed, many US congresspersons were wary because they feared it would

Secret Service agents walk alongside the carriage carrying US president Theodore Roosevelt at his inauguration in Washington, DC, in 1905.

accelerate the investigation of corruption in Congress, which had begun under the Secret Service. As a result, the bureau was authorized by an executive order of President Theodore Roosevelt, not by an act of Congress. Its early duties were investigating antitrust cases, crimes committed on government property, and crimes committed by government officials.

In 1920, the Department of the Treasury created the first sizable federal police agency. The "T-Men," as they came to be known, were charged with enforcing Prohibition—the nationwide ban on the manufacture, sale, and transportation of alcohol. The force grew to a force of approximately 4,000 officers during the peak of the government's fight against alcohol.

During the early twentieth century, some states began to create police forces, as other states (such

New York City police officers oversee the disposal of illegal liquor during the Prohibition era.

as Texas and Massachusetts) had done on a smaller scale before. In 1905, Pennsylvania established the first modern state police department. Formed with the professed purpose of fighting rural crime, state police in Pennsylvania were used mostly to work around corrupt or inefficient local police forces and to control strikes in areas where local police were sympathetic to unions. Other states soon followed Pennsylvania's lead.

REFORM EFFORTS

Efforts to reform policing during the late nineteenth and early twentieth centuries came from both outside and inside the police system. They aimed for the creation of professional police forces led by experts responsible to a public authority that was free of political influence. During this period, the Boston Police Department, under Commissioner Stephen James O'Meara, came closest to that ideal. O'Meara was a strong leader who created a high standard of integrity and legality in his department. As a result of his example, the strong chief executive as an agent of change became a characteristic of police agencies in other cities. In 1919, however, O'Meara's legacy was spoiled when most of Boston's police officers went on strike after they were denied the right to form a union. The episode, known as the Boston Police Strike, led to a crime wave and devastated the city's police department.

Massachusetts governor Calvin Coolidge *(right)* inspects state militia called in to help quell the Boston Police Strike of 1919. His role in ending the strike brought Coolidge to national prominence, and he rose to the presidency in 1923.

Prohibition was one factor motivating police reform in the United States in the 1920s and early 1930s. The alcohol ban led to a vast black market in the major cities and to the rise of powerful criminal gangs that corrupted and intimidated political leaders and police. There was a corresponding decline of public confidence in the police.

VOLLMER AND THE SOCIAL ROLE OF POLICE

The founder of the professional policing reform movement in the United States was August Vollmer. Beginning his career in 1905 as the head of a six-person police department in Berkeley, California, Vollmer ultimately developed a model of policing that had national influence. He applied concepts from the study of management, sociology, social work, psychology, and technology to policing, and he was the first major police official to argue that police officers should have a college education. In 1916, Vollmer helped to create the first university-level police educational program in the United States at the University of California, Berkeley.

Vollmer also believed that the police should have a social function in addition to their traditional law-enforcement role. He thought that the police could play a role in upholding such social institutions as the family, churches, schools, and neighborhoods. For example, he argued that special juvenile bureaus should be created

August Vollmer

to handle problems of children and families and that police should work more closely with social agencies.

In addition to giving police an ideal to strive toward, Vollmer also helped transform the International Association of Chiefs of Police, founded in 1893, into a truly national police organization. Within this organization he created the Uniform Crime Reports program, which became (after it was taken over by the FBI in 1930) an important indicator of the annual national crime rate and of the performance of local police departments. Finally, through his work on the Wickersham Commission, which was set up to examine law enforcement in the era of Prohibition, Vollmer exposed many unconstitutional police practices—particularly the use of torture in the interrogation of suspects—to public scrutiny.

J. EDGAR HOOVER AND THE CRIME-FIGHTING MODEL

At the federal level, the FBI was professionalized under the leadership of J. Edgar Hoover. Named director in 1924, Hoover thoroughly reorganized the bureau and made it into the most efficient police and investigative force in the world. The public's opinion of detectives was ready for change. Inspired by detective-heroes in popular novels and short stories, the American public developed a new interest in real-life accounts of detective work. Hoover set out to make the fictional image of the detective into reality.

Hoover eliminated corruption by suspending bureau investigations requiring considerable undercover or investigative work and by creating a strong bureaucracy that emphasized accountability. He established the FBI Identification Division in 1924 to keep extensive fingerprint records. The FBI crime laboratory was created in 1932 to provide scientific crime-detection facilities, and the FBI National Academy was opened in 1935 for training local law-enforcement officials.

J. Edgar Hoover

Under Hoover's influence, police work moved away from Vollmer's emphasis on social work toward a narrower focus on fighting serious street crimes. The new police reformers also moved to sever the close ties between officers and neighborhoods. Assignments were changed often; officers no longer patrolled areas in which they lived; and, most important, the police began to patrol in automobiles. This crime-fighting model came to dominate policing in the United States. After World Wars I and II, as American political influence grew, the model was adopted in other countries.

FURTHER DEVELOPMENTS UNDER WILSON

Ironically, it was Vollmer's protégé, Orlando W. Wilson, who became the architect of the crime-fighting model. Through various posts as chief of police, superintendent of police, and professor of criminology, Wilson supported the development of crime-focused police departments. He also promoted the use of motorized patrol units and radio communication systems, which enabled rapid responses to calls for assistance. Wilson's strategy of policing came to fruition during the 1960s.

Despite its initial promise, the crime-fighting model had many drawbacks. It greatly reduced the role of citizens in preventing crime in their neighborhoods. In

The use of patrol vehicles in policing became common in the 1950s. In this photograph, police officers arrest a man for disorderly conduct in Greenville, South Carolina.

addition, the motorization of police patrols isolated officers from the communities and citizens they served. Police interacted with citizens mostly in situations where a crime had been committed and officers were expected to take action to enforce the law. Those often negative encounters tended to increase hostility between police and citizens, especially in minority communities.

Meanwhile, in Britain, foot patrols continued in most cities, which lacked the suburban "sprawl" of American cities. Although the American rapid-response model had some influence in Britain, it was counterbalanced by the continued emphasis on the "neighborhood bobby."

THE CRISIS OF POLICING

In the 1960s and 1970s, policing in the United States underwent a crisis. Despite massive spending for more officers, crime rates continued to rise. In the 1960s, hundreds of urban riots and violent demonstrations occurred. Minority groups, especially African Americans, resented the harsh tactics used by police. Meanwhile, police violence against protesters in civil rights and antiwar demonstrations—some of which were broadcast on live television—caused public outrage.

In 1967, President Lyndon B. Johnson created a national commission to study the causes of urban riots throughout the country. The commission found the ultimate cause was racism. Furthermore, the commission found that violent police tactics often made the riots worse. Yet, despite the violence in such cities as Los Angeles, Chicago, New York City, and Detroit, it can fairly be said that during this period the fear of crime escalated more rapidly than crime itself. Many citizens took measures to defend themselves and their homes. Many left the cities for the suburbs.

In the late twentieth century, Britain also faced urban riots in minority communities. In 1981, a government

On May 3, 1963, police officers in Birmingham, Alabama, use police dogs to attack a civil rights protester. Police responses to urban riots and civil rights protests in the 1960s had a negative impact on the public's view of the police.

report concluded that police had become too remote from their communities, that local citizens should have more input into police policy making, and that police tactics should be more sensitive to the growing cultural diversity of Britain's major cities. At the same time, the report endorsed the traditional view that the primary duty of the police is to maintain public order. Nevertheless, periodic rioting continued to plague such cities as Bristol, Birmingham, and Bradford in the last decades of the twentieth century.

In response to the crisis in policing, research studies were undertaken. In the 1950s and 1960s, both civilian and police groups had assumed that the main activity of police officers was fighting crime (by making arrests, for example). However, studies showed that crime fighting actually made up less than one-fifth of patrol activities. The remainder included resolving conflicts, providing emergency services, and maintaining order. Citizens often called on the police to perform tasks not specified in the law.

American studies of the effectiveness of automobile patrols found that, despite taking up substantial amounts of police time, relatively little crime-fighting activity resulted directly from police patrols. More than nine-tenths of arrests, for example, resulted from citizens' requests for police action. Later studies found that preventive patrols by automobile did not effectively reduce crime, increase public satisfaction with police, or decrease citizens' fear of crime. Moreover, during the late 1970s, several studies on the effectiveness of rapid response to calls for service found that it did little to prevent crime. Such findings led to an increased questioning of the crime-fighting model of policing and helped to bring about a period of experimentation.

DUE PROCESS AND INDIVIDUAL RIGHTS

Just as the dominant model of policing was being challenged, the US Supreme Court began a "rights revolution" that put greater restrictions on police searches and interrogations. In the 1960s, the court issued a series of rulings on due process that applied the Bill of Rights to state actions. Under Chief Justice Earl Warren, the court continued to support the autonomy of law-enforcement officials while also asserting that suspects have a right to fair treatment.

The court's ruling in the case *Mapp v. Ohio* (1961) prevented prosecutors from using evidence seized in illegal searches. In *Escobedo v. Illinois* (1964), the court held that a suspect is entitled to have a lawyer present during interrogation at a police station and that denying a suspect's request for a lawyer makes any statements a suspect makes inadmissible in court. In the landmark case *Miranda v. Arizona* (1966), the court established a number of new guidelines for police interrogations.

Earl Warren, chief justice of the US Supreme Court from 1953 to 1969

MIRANDA V. ARIZONA

Perhaps the most famous phrase heard in police dramas is, "You have the right to remain silent..." The expression originated with a US Supreme Court case decided on June 13, 1966. The case, *Miranda v. Arizona*, specified a code of conduct for police questioning criminal suspects held in custody. Chief Justice Earl Warren, writing for the majority of the justices, ruled that prosecutors may not use statements made by a person during interrogation unless certain procedural safeguards were followed. The court detailed a statement of rights, known as the Miranda warnings, that must be read to arrested persons prior to questioning. Suspects must be told that they have the right to remain silent and that anything they say may be used against them as evidence. They must also be told that they have the right to have an attorney present and that if they cannot afford an attorney, one will be appointed for them.

The Miranda ruling was one of the most controversial decisions of the Warren Court, which had become increasingly concerned about the methods used by local police to obtain confessions. Critics of the Miranda decision argued that the court, in seeking to protect the rights of individuals, had seriously weakened law enforcement. Later decisions by the Supreme Court limited some of the potential scope of the Miranda safeguards.

In 2000, the Supreme Court decided *Dickerson v. United States*, a case concerning the Miranda warnings. With only two dissenters, the court declined to overrule the Miranda decision.

The rulings made in these cases directly affected the day-to-day activities of police. They also helped improve the professionalism of police officers. Police departments nationwide reacted to their increased liability by raising recruitment standards, improving legal training for officers, and establishing procedures for officers to follow in the handling and arresting of suspects.

COMMUNITY POLICING

Meanwhile, the limitations of the crime-fighting model led police departments to look to alternative strategies. Many departments sought to increase their effectiveness by improving their relationships with the communities they served. In the 1980s and 1990s, an increasing number of departments began using an approach known as community policing.

EARLY COMMUNITY OUTREACH MODELS

Beginning in the 1940s, some police departments created communication and education programs for communities with racial minorities. One goal of such programs was to help police understand and overcome their prejudice toward minorities and thereby improve their treatment of those groups. Although the programs drew support from community and social-justice organizations, most of them took the form of specialized community-relations units staffed by minority officers. With little support from police officers, the programs eventually turned into public-relations efforts aimed at overcoming community dissatisfaction with police tactics. The failure of these programs was made apparent by the violent clashes between police and minority groups in the riots of the 1960s.

Team policing was introduced in the early 1970s in New York City. This approach emphasized the delivery of round-the-clock patrol services by a team of officers in a specific geographic area. Team commanders were responsible for conditions in the patrol area, regardless of whether they were on duty. It was hoped that the assignment of fixed neighborhoods to the teams would break down barriers between residents and police and that police could provide services better suited to the residents' needs. In turn, the job satisfaction of officers was expected to rise. However, studies of the effectiveness of team policing in several cities in the United States failed to show any improvement over the crime-fighting model. Resistance within police departments and inadequate training brought team policing to an end by the mid-1970s.

THE GROWTH OF COMMUNITY POLICING

During this period, the complex role of police in society came into clearer focus. Police administrators and researchers maintained that police deal with many behaviors that are not defined as criminal and that many police tasks concerning noncriminal behavior are as important as their traditional tasks of enforcing public order. They emphasized that police must be allowed discretion in carrying out their duties (particularly regarding whether to arrest a suspect) and that a police force that is not in close contact with its community will have difficulty controlling crime and disorder. Finally, they acknowledged that police must be accountable to elected officials and to the public.

This new wisdom led in the 1980s to the gradual replacement of the crime-fighting model by the set of strategies and programs known as community policing. The basic premise of community policing is that the police should involve the community in their efforts to prevent and control crime and to solve communitywide problems. Community policing departs from the crime-fighting model by making the police officer a neighborhood problem solver rather than an incident-driven crime fighter. Police officers assigned to community-policing duties are expected to maintain close contact with the community and to become familiar with its residents and its problems through foot patrols, community meetings, and service at police substations. The same familiarity with the community is also expected of police administrators.

Those who support community policing believe that the approach makes use of various resources to solve problems that affect community safety and stability over the long term. They also argue that the traditional crime-fighting model of policing lets problems worsen, as it simply responds to incidents as they occur instead of addressing the underlying causes of crime.

RESEARCH ON COMMUNITY POLICING

A large body of research supported the move toward community policing. In the hugely influential article "Broken Windows: The Police and Neighborhood Safety" (1982), the American political scientist James Q. Wilson and the American criminologist George L. Kelling linked the occurrence and fear of crime to the existence of disorderly conditions in neighborhoods. Using the metaphor of a broken window, they argued that a building in disrepair looks as though it has been abandoned; this encourages criminals to damage it further. As the building is eventually destroyed, nearby residents grow less concerned about their neighborhood and community, which leads to an increase in disorderly behavior. Such behavior in turn creates public fear and encourages those can afford it to leave the neighborhood. With time, crime continues to increase and the neighborhood becomes unlivable for those who stay. According to Wilson and Kelling, the crime-fighting model of policing ignores the law-enforcement equivalent of broken windows.

On January 19, 2012, George Kelling, coauthor of the influential 1982 article "Broken Windows," and Detroit police chief Ralph Godbee discuss the implementation of the "broken windows" policing strategy in Detroit.

Wilson and Kelling argued that police departments should use patrol tactics designed to counteract disorder and to preserve the community in troubled neighborhoods. The visibility of police in those areas

discourages potential criminals and generates goodwill among law-abiding citizens, who are encouraged to assert control over public spaces. The problem of crime and community safety become the joint responsibilities of both residents and police.

COMMUNITY POLICING FROM THE 1990S TO THE PRESENT

In the 1990s, community policing became part of a national strategy to combat crime in the United States. A law passed in 1994 provided for the hiring of 100,000 new community police officers and set up the Office of Community Oriented Policing Services, overseen by the Department of Justice. By the early twenty-first century, about two-thirds of local police departments in the United States, employing some nine-tenths of the country's police officers, had some type of community-policing plan. In many police departments, organized subunits, rather than the entire police force, carried out community policing.

Despite its widespread adoption, community policing has faced obstacles. Some police administrators have been reluctant to support programs that require officers on the street to use considerable discretion and authority, especially in departments where officers are not well prepared to identify and address complex community problems. Other administrators have continued to believe that the more traditional crime-fighting model, despite its flaws, is still an effective overall policing strategy.

COMPSTAT

In the late twentieth century, police agencies throughout the United States and in parts of Britain began adopting computerized systems known as CompStat (short for "computerized statistics"). Such systems could be used to plot specific incidents of crime by time, day, and location. By revealing previously unnoticed crime patterns, CompStat enabled police departments to allocate their resources more effectively. Several of the cities in which it was used credited CompStat with significant decreases in crime rates. CompStat became so widely used in the United States that many police administrators began to regard it as the basis of a new model of policing for the twenty-first century. Thus far, however, CompStat has been a useful supplement to the existing crime-fighting and community-policing models.

Chapter Four

THE 21ST CENTURY: COUNTERTERRORISM AND RACIAL TENSIONS

In the early twenty-first century, two factors have greatly changed the nature and strategies of policing: terrorism and racial tensions between police and minorities. The former has been a factor on an international scale, while the latter largely has been a domestic issue in the United States. Both have led to close examinations of the role of the police in protecting communities and have shown the crucial need for careful oversight of law enforcement.

POLICE AND COUNTERTERRORISM

Although police worldwide had been combating terrorism long before 2001, the magnitude of the September 11 attacks against the United States and of subsequent acts of terrorism in other countries (including Spain, Britain, France, Morocco, and Egypt) showed that conventional tactics were no longer adequate. Police departments would have to work more closely with national security agencies, and many police resources would have to be redirected toward the surveillance of suspected terrorists.

From about 1960 to about 1980, police in Europe and North America confronted a wave of terrorism that swept over several countries. Although some of the organizations involved still exist, police eliminated most of them, including the Front de Libération du Québec in Canada, the Red Army Faction in what was then West Germany, and the Red Brigades in Italy. The police owed their success mostly to their ability to infiltrate the terrorist networks with human sources, who then worked with informants.

To a large extent, police used the same methods against terrorism that they had successfully used in certain countries against organized crime. They were at times granted emergency powers that allowed them to detain suspects for longer periods for questioning.

Some countries also enacted policies against terrorist sympathizers, such as the Berufsverbot ("work ban") in West Germany, which prohibited a person identified as a sympathizer from working in government service. Police operatives also resorted to various tricks of questionable legality, such as break-ins, intimidation, the publication of fake terrorist communications, the spread of false rumors about individuals, and entrapment. Various commissions investigated and made those abuses public.

After the September 11 attacks, it was recognized that the nature of terrorism had changed and that corresponding changes were needed in counterterrorism tactics. First, terrorism was harder to combat. Because terrorism had become truly global, the languages and customs of terrorists often differed from those of local police, making infiltration more difficult. Moreover, although the community-policing movement had helped police develop closer ties to the communities they served, in some cases it also created feelings of loyalty that discouraged police from sharing information about their communities with intelligence agencies. Second, the scale of devastation caused by terrorist attacks such as those of September 11 made the attacks seem more like acts of war than crimes. Especially in the United States, terrorism was considered a military problem as well as a law-enforcement problem. This made it more difficult to develop effective policing strategies against terrorists.

Shown here is the aftermath of the December 30, 2006, terrorist attack by the Basque separatist group ETA at an airport in Madrid, Spain. In the twenty-first century, counter-terrorism has become a major focus of law-enforcement agencies worldwide.

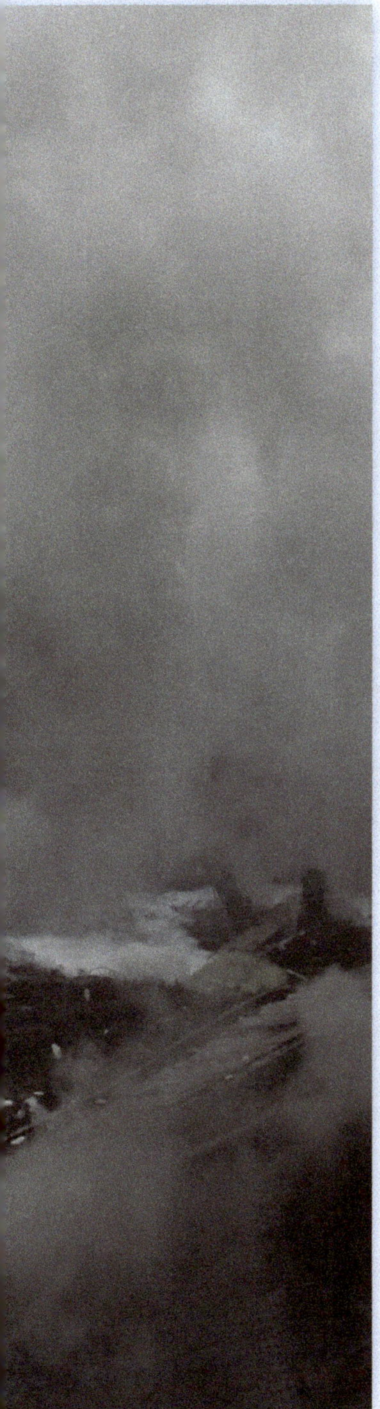

It is widely accepted that police and national intelligence agencies must cooperate in investigations of terrorism. However, such cooperation has been impeded by long-standing institutional barriers. Police detectives and intelligence agents often do not share common goals: police aim at swiftly prosecuting an offender, whereas intelligence agents continue collecting information until they can wipe out whole terrorist networks. The so-called "wall" between law-enforcement agencies, such as the FBI, and the intelligence community is no myth. The sharing of information is made even more difficult by the fact that members of local police agencies, whose contributions may be vital, may not hold the proper security clearance needed for access to sensitive intelligence. Such problems are only magnified when the law-enforcement and intelligence agencies involved are located in different countries.

THE USA PATRIOT ACT

Following the September 11 terrorist attacks, law-enforcement agencies, lawmakers, and the American public questioned the effectiveness of the country's counterterrorism techniques. President George W. Bush responded to the attacks by calling for a global war on terrorism. In October 2001, as part of a broad attempt to expand intelligence and surveillance programs, Congress passed the USA PATRIOT Act (in full, the Uniting and Strengthening America by Providing Appropriate Tools Required to Intercept and Obstruct Terrorism

US president George W. Bush addresses the American public on September 11, 2001.

Act). This act gave the Federal Bureau of Investigation (FBI) and other law-enforcement agencies wide powers of search and surveillance in pursuing suspected terrorists, including great leeway in eavesdropping and detaining suspects.

The act drew widespread criticism from civil liberties advocates, who charged that several parts of the statute were unconstitutional or invited abuse by federal authorities. Section 215, for example, allegedly violated the right to privacy established by the Fourth Amendment because it allowed law enforcement to conduct warrantless searches and did not require notification of the target, even after the search had taken place. Similarly, Section 218 effectively allowed the FBI to conduct surveillance of US citizens without showing probable cause of criminal activity.

In 2013, Edward Snowden, an American intelligence contractor, revealed that the National Security Agency (NSA) was using Section 215 of the PATRIOT Act to collect the phone records of millions of Americans not under investigation for terrorism. In June 2015, Congress allowed Section 215, along with other provisions of the act, to expire. A new law, the USA Freedom Act, renewed those provisions, but Section 215 was substantially revised to end the NSA's data-gathering program. Privacy-rights groups applauded the change.

On July 7, 2005, London police officers respond to a series of terrorist bomb attacks on the city's transit system. Significant police resources—especially in major cities—are dedicated to combating terrorism.

The surveillance and arrest of terrorist suspects—as well as preparation for future terrorist attacks—require significant police manpower and resources. As a result, some people fear that the police reform programs put in place since the 1980s will lose funding and come to a halt.

TENSIONS WITH MINORITY GROUPS

The other factor that has greatly affected policing and public attitudes toward the police in recent years has been tensions between police and minorities. A number of incidents made national headlines and led to widespread protests against racial profiling, police brutality, and the use of deadly force, particularly against African Americans.

SHOOTING OF TRAYVON MARTIN

The incident that brought renewed attention to the strained relations between law enforcement and minorities was the fatal shooting of Trayvon Martin, a seventeen-year-old African American in Sanford, Florida, in February 2012. The shooting revealed deep divisions among Americans on race issues.

Martin was walking home from a convenience store when he was noticed by George Zimmerman, a white neighborhood-watch volunteer. Zimmerman called the local police department to report Martin as a suspicious person. Although the dispatcher told Zimmerman that he should not follow Martin, Zimmerman left his vehicle. A violent confrontation followed, and Zimmerman shot Martin at close range, killing him. When police arrived, Zimmerman argued that he had been assaulted by Martin, who was unarmed, and that he fired in self-defense. Police did not arrest Zimmerman because no evidence contradicted his version of the event and because the use of deadly force in self-defense is legal in Florida.

In the following weeks, Zimmerman remained free as the shooting drew increasing media attention. The lack of criminal charges against Zimmerman was seen by many as an injustice, and demonstrations demanding his prosecution for murder were organized in cities across the United States. In April 2012 the governor of Florida appointed a special prosecutor for the case, who brought a criminal charge of second-degree murder against Zimmerman.

Zimmerman's trial in 2013 received intensive media coverage. Prosecutors argued that Martin's death was racially motivated. The defense argued that evidence backed up Zimmerman's claim that he fired his weapon in self-defense. Central elements of the incident, however, could not be determined with clarity. On July 13, 2013, the jury declared Zimmerman not guilty.

Martin's death caused an intense debate over race relations in the United States. Although Zimmerman was not a police officer, his actions and trial brought increased scrutiny to the practice of racial profiling in law enforcement. Protests across the United States in the wake of the Zimmerman verdict led to the formation of the Black Lives Matter social movement, which focused on better treatment of African Americans in all facets of American society.

POLICE VIOLENCE AGAINST AFRICAN AMERICANS

Amid the national conversation about race following the Trayvon Martin shooting, a series of high-profile incidents brought the issue of police violence against African Americans to the headlines. Widespread outrage over these incidents fueled the growth of the Black Lives Matter movement.

In August 2014, Michael Brown, an unarmed African American teenager, was fatally shot by Darren Wilson, a white police officer in Ferguson, Missouri. Days

Members of the Black Lives Matter movement protest in St. Louis, Missouri, in November 2014 in response to the fatal police shooting of Michael Brown.

of civil unrest and protests broke out, drawing national and international attention. A few months later, in

November, a white police officer in Cleveland, Ohio, fatally shot a twelve-year-old African American child who held a pellet gun in a public park. The immediacy with which the officer fired his weapon upon arrival at the park reinforced popular perception that the shooting was unjustified and racially motivated.

In December 2014, a grand jury failed to indict a New York City police officer for his role in the death of Eric Garner, an unarmed African American man who died after having a choke hold applied to him during his arrest for a nonviolent crime on Staten Island in July. President Obama and New York City mayor Bill de Blasio then set up a task force charged with improving relations between minority communities and police. However, many of those around the country who had taken to the streets to proclaim that "black lives matter" felt that not enough was being done.

Protesters' allegations seemed confirmed by further violent encounters between law-enforcement officials and African Americans. In April 2015, a young African American man in Baltimore, Maryland, named Freddie Gray died a week after suffering a severe spinal-cord injury while

Protests and riots broke out in Baltimore, Maryland, in 2015 following Freddie Gray's death while in police custody. Here, a protester *(left)* argues with a police officer who is attempting to uphold a citywide curfew.

in police custody. Rioting erupted in Baltimore on the day of his funeral. In July 2015, Sandra Bland, a twenty-eight-year-old African American woman,

was pulled over for a minor traffic violation in Texas. While in police custody, Bland was found dead. A grand jury failed to indict anyone in connection with Bland's death. In November 2015, there was an uproar in Chicago following the court-ordered release of a video showing a police officer shooting and killing an African American teenager in October 2014.

These incidents have led to increased scrutiny of the qualifications of police officers and the techniques they use to fight crime. Perhaps the greatest challenge faced by law-enforcement agencies in the twenty-first century is accountability and oversight. As technology such as smartphones and body cameras bring more visibility to the actions of police officers, public pressure for reform will likely grow.

CONCLUSION

The Roman poet Juvenal posed the question *Quis custodiet ipsos custodes?* ("Who guards the guardians?") in the second century CE, and the cautionary quotation remains relevant nearly two thousand years later. After Juvenal's time, the rise of the modern nation saw the development of the state monopoly on violence, the belief that only the legitimate government of a country has the right to use physical force within its borders. This maxim has its limits, however, and other hallmarks of a modern free society, such as the rule of law and due process, are intended to regulate the actions of the state against its citizens. Thus, the statement "To serve and protect" contains an inherent tension, as the methods that one would use to "serve" a society might not be those that would most effectively "protect" it, and vice versa. The push and pull between respect for personal liberty and the desire to fight crime has led to discussions about the role of law enforcement, the boundaries within which police officers operate, and the very real threats that police officers face on a daily basis.

3000 BCE The first policing organization is created in Egypt.

7 BCE Augustus divides Rome into fourteen administrative wards, each overseen by a magistrate.

1066 William, duke of Normandy, leads the Norman Conquest of England. The Norman rulers would soon introduce the office of constable to England's justice system.

1285 The Statute of Winchester codifies England's system of social obligation.

1536–1544 King Francis I creates the first policing system in France, the *maréchaussée*.

1666 King Louis XIV of France centralizes Parisian police forces and establishes the office of lieutenant of police.

1749 Henry and John Fielding create the Bow Street Runners, a salaried body of constables.

1786 The Dublin Police Act creates a professional police force in Dublin, Ireland.

1796 The Ministry of Police is created in France.

1798 The Thames River Police is created in England.

1829 The Metropolitan Police Act establishes the London Metropolitan Police Department.

1833 The Sydney Police Act establishes city police forces in Australia.

1835 The Municipal Corporations Act orders all English boroughs to set up police forces.

1835–1840 City police departments are established in the Canadian cities of Toronto, Quebec, and Montreal.

1842 The London Metropolitan Police Department establishes the first detective branch (later the Criminal Investigations Department).

1844 The first police department in the United States is established in New York City.

1850 Allan Pinkerton creates the Pinkerton National Detective Agency, an independent police force.

1856 The County and Borough Police Act mandates provincial police forces throughout England.

1865 The United States Secret Service is established.

1867 Provincial polices forces are established in Canada.

1873 The North West Mounted Police (later renamed the Royal Canadian Mounted Police) is created to police western Canada.

1908 The Bureau of Investigation (later the Federal Bureau of Investigation, or FBI) is established in the United States.

1916 The first university-level police educational program is created at the University of California, Berkeley.

1924 J. Edgar Hoover becomes head of the Bureau of Investigation.

1950 Orlando W. Wilson's *Police Administration*, for many years considered the bible of American policing, is published.

1960s Widespread urban riots and clashes with police undermine the public image of police officers in the United States. A series of US Supreme Court decisions place new restrictions on police searches and interrogations.

1994 The US Violent Crime Control and Law Enforcement Act is passed.

2001 Following the September 11 terrorist attacks against the United States, law-enforcement agencies and intelligence agencies begin coordinating counterterrorism efforts.

2010s A series of incidents in which African American suspects are fatally shot by police or die in police custody spawns substantial media coverage and public scrutiny of law-enforcement techniques.

GLOSSARY

ACCOUNTABILITY An obligation or willingness to accept responsibility or to account for one's actions.

BLACK MARKET A system through which things are bought and sold illegally.

BOBBY British term for a police officer.

BUREAU A government department or part of a government department in the United States.

BUREAUCRACY A large group of people who are involved in running a government but who are not elected.

COMMISSIONER The officer in charge of a department or bureau of the public service.

CONSTABLE A public official whose job is similar to that of a police officer but who is elected or appointed rather than hired.

DUE PROCESS The rule that a legal case must be done in a way that protects the rights of all the people involved.

ENTRAPMENT The illegal act of tricking someone into committing a crime so that the person you have tricked can be arrested.

FRANKPLEDGE A system in medieval England under which each adult male member of a tithing was responsible for the good conduct of the others.

GRATUITY An amount of money given to a person who has performed a service.

INADMISSIBLE Not able to be allowed or considered in a legal case.

INFILTRATE To secretly enter or join something (such as a group or an organization) to get information or do harm.

INFORMANT A person who gives information to the police about secret or criminal activities.

INTERROGATION The formal questioning of someone in a thorough and often forceful way.

INTIMIDATION Actions taken to compel or deter by or as if by threats.

MAGISTRATE A local official exercising administrative and often judicial functions.

NOME A province of ancient Egypt.

PREVENTIVE Done to keep something from happening.

PROCEDURAL Of or relating to the procedure used by courts or other bodies administering substantive law.

PROHIBITION The period of time from 1920 to 1933 in the United States when it was illegal to make or sell alcohol.

SHIRE A county in England.

TITHING A small administrative division preserved in parts of England that was originally made up of ten men and their families.

UNCONSTITUTIONAL Not allowed by the constitution of a country or government.

FOR MORE INFORMATION

Canadian Police College (CPC)
PO Box 8900
Ottawa, ON K1G 3J2
Canada
(613) 993-9501
Website: https://www.cpc.gc.ca/en

The CPC is responsible for training law-enforcement officials throughout Canada. Its library (https://www.cpc.gc.ca/en/library) holds an extensive collection of publications on the Canadian police community.

City of London Police Museum
Wood Street Police Station
37 Wood Street
London EC2P 2NQ
United Kingdom
Website: https://www.cityoflondon.police.uk/about-us/history/museum

The City of London Police Museum's collection provides insight into the development of policing in the United Kingdom from its earliest days through the present.

Federal Bureau of Investigation (FBI)
FBI Headquarters
935 Pennsylvania Avenue NW
Washington, DC 20535

(202) 324-3000
Website: https://www.fbi.gov

The FBI is the main investigative agency of the federal government of the United States. It is responsible for conducting investigations in cases where federal laws may have been violated. The FBI website provides resources for students on the bureau's history and operations.

Illinois State Police (ISP) Heritage Foundation Museum
4000 North Peoria Road
Springfield, IL 62702
(217) 525-1922
Website: http://www.isphf.org

Opened in 2005, the ISP Heritage Foundation Museum is dedicated to preserving the history of the Illinois State Police. In 2016, it began construction on the ISP Memorial Park in Springfield, Illinois.

Los Angeles Police Museum (LAPM)
6045 York Boulevard
Los Angeles, CA 90042
(323) 344-9445
Website: http://www.laphs.org

The LAPM documents the history of the Los Angeles Police Department (LAPD). It preserves and displays vehicles, weapons, uniforms, and other artifacts of the LAPD.

Phoenix Police Museum
17 South 2nd Avenue
Historic City Hall, 1st Floor
Phoenix, AZ 85003
(602) 534-7278
Website: http://phoenixpolicemuseum.org

The Phoenix Police Museum hosts engaging exhibits on the history of the Phoenix Police Department. Topics include the Arizona Rangers, developments in police technology, and the landmark Supreme Court case *Miranda v. Arizona*.

Royal Canadian Mounted Police (RCMP) Heritage Centre
5907 Dewdney Avenue
Regina, SK S4T 0P4
Canada
(866) 567-7267
Website: http://www.rcmphc.com

The RCMP Heritage Centre promotes the heritage of Canada's iconic Mounties. Its exhibits cover the history of the RCMP from its formation to today.

WEBSITES

Because of the changing nature of internet links, Rosen Publishing has developed an online list of websites related to the subject of this book. This site is updated regularly. Please use this link to access the list:

http://www.rosenlinks.com/BLAW/serve

FOR FURTHER READING

Aronson, Marc. *Master of Deceit: J. Edgar Hoover and America in the Age of Lies*. Somerville, MA: Candlewick Press, 2012.

Bowman, Chris. *Police Officer* (Dangerous Jobs). Minneapolis, MN: Bellwether Media, 2015.

Collard, Sneed B. *The CIA and FBI: Top Secret*. Vero Beach, FL: Rourke Educational Media, 2014.

Espejo, Roman. *Community Policing* (Opposing Viewpoints). Farmington Hills, MI: Greenhaven Press, 2014.

Greve, Tom. *Police: Protect and Serve*. Vero Beach, FL: Rourke Educational Media, 2015.

Merino, Noël. *Civil Liberties* (Opposing Viewpoints). Farmington Hills, MI: Greenhaven Press, 2013.

Seiple, Samantha. *Lincoln's Spymaster: Allan Pinkerton, America's First Private Eye*. New York, NY: Scholastic Press, 2015.

Sutherland, Adam. *Police Forensics* (On the Radar: Defend and Protect). Minneapolis, MN: Lerner Publications, 2012.

Vander Hook, Sue. *Miranda v. Arizona: An Individual's Rights When Under Arrest*. Minneapolis, MN: ABDO Publishing, 2013.

Woog, Adam. *Careers in the FBI*. New York, NY: Cavendish Square Publishing, 2014.

Woog, Adam. *Careers in State, County, and City Police Forces*. New York, NY: Cavendish Square Publishing, 2014.